The REAL TEST

Fifteen great
SHARP SHADES 2.0 *reads:*

The REAL TEST

Jill Atkins

Ransom

SHARP SHADES 2.0
The Real Test
by Jill Atkins

Published by Ransom Publishing Ltd.
Unit 7, Brocklands Farm, West Meon, Hampshire GU32 1JN, UK
www.ransom.co.uk

ISBN   978 178127 981 6
First published in 2016

Copyright © 2016 Ransom Publishing Ltd.
Text copyright © 2016 Jill Atkins
Cover photograph copyright © filo. Other images copyright © IPGGutenbergUKLtd;
Bplanet; eyecrave; Peter Zelei; Juanmonino; jcjgphotography; kycstudio; mmz; MrJub;
Barcin.

A CIP catalogue record of this book is available from the British Library.

All rights reserved. No part of this publication may be reproduced, stored in a
retrieval system, or transmitted, in any form or by any means, electronic, mechanical,
photocopying, recording or otherwise, without the prior permission of the publishers.

The right of Jill Atkins to be identified as the author of this Work has been
asserted by her in accordance with sections 77 and 78 of the Copyright, Design and
Patents Act 1988.

CONTENTS

ONE

Ryan grinned as he made his way home. It had been a cinch. He couldn't wait to tell the crowd.

'Hi, Ryan!'

Ryan froze mid-step. He knew

that voice. It was Mollie. He looked across the road. Wow! There she was, as stunning as ever.

'Did you pass?' Mollie called.

'Yeah!' he shouted.

'Great!' Mollie dashed across the road. She gave him a hug. He felt his knees buckle and his head spin.

He would never forget the day he first saw her at the club. She was dancing. It felt like he had been struck by lightning.

Mollie smiled up at him.

'So, when do we get to go out in your car?' she asked.

Ryan smiled back.

'My mum's car, you mean,' he said, trying to look cool.

'Your mum's car, then,' said Mollie, as they began to walk along the road.

She doesn't seem to mind. She just wants to be with me.

'She'll let me use it any time I want,' he lied.

'Great!'

'So what are you doing tonight?' asked Ryan. 'We can go anywhere you like.'

If Mum will let me.

They reached Ryan's house and burst in at the back door. His

younger brother, Kev, and his best
mate, Jordan, were in the kitchen.

'I passed!' shouted Ryan.

'You jammy devil!' laughed Kev.
'You must have brown-nosed!'

Everyone laughed.

'No!' said Ryan. 'I was just
brilliant.'

'So when do we get to see your
perfect driving?' asked Jordan.

'We're all going out in his mum's
car tonight,' said Mollie.

'You're on!' said Jordan.

Ryan frowned. He thought maybe
Mollie wanted a date, but perhaps it
was only the car she was interested

in. He looked at her and she smiled again. He felt his heart miss a beat. Then he heard Kev laugh.

'I'll bet you a fiver Mum won't let you drive the car,' said Kev.

Ryan wished Kev hadn't said that. Not in front of Jordan and Mollie. He punched his brother's shoulder.

'She'll let me have the car,' he said. 'I'll be five quid better off by tonight.'

But he wished he could be so sure.

TWO

Ryan was mad.

As soon as Mum had come in from work, he had made her a cup of tea.

'I passed!' he said.

'Well done!' she said, but she didn't sound that excited.

He took a deep breath. 'So can I have the car tonight?'

'No,' she said.

'Why not?'

'I'm going round to Helen's,' said Mum. 'So I need the car.'

'But I've promised my mates,' he shouted.

'Well, you'll have to un-promise them, won't you?'

Ryan was disgusted. He stormed out of the room and stomped up to his bedroom. It was just his luck to have such a mean mother.

A few moments later, the bedroom door flew open. Kev stood in the doorway, grinning. Ryan knew what his rotten brother had come for.

'My fiver,' said Kev, holding out his hand.

Ryan slapped the note onto his brother's hand. He said nothing. He was too angry.

'Easy money,' laughed Kev, as he backed out of the room.

Ryan sat down on his bed. How was he going to tell Jordan? Jordan would make him the laughing stock of the crowd.

Even worse, Mollie wouldn't go out with a nerd who was under his mum's thumb.

He decided to call Jordan first.

'I'm not having the car after all tonight,' he said.

Jordan laughed. 'So Kev was right! Mummy won't let you have it!'

'It's not like that,' Ryan lied. 'I'm saving the Big Night Out for the weekend. Let's hang out down the club tonight.'

Ryan heard a snigger. Would Jordan give him hell?

It wasn't so easy telling Mollie.

'Er … Mollie,' he muttered down the phone.

'Hi, Ryan.' She sounded pleased it was him. His heart sunk to his boots.

'I thought … ' he stuttered, ' … it would be cool … if we all met down the club tonight.'

'Oh.'

'We could do the car thing at the weekend.'

'All right,' she said, but her voice had lost its brightness.

He felt like killing his mum.

The evening was a disaster. Jordan

kept telling everyone about it.
But worse than that, Mollie didn't
even turn up!

THREE

By the end of the week, Ryan still hadn't used the car. And he hadn't seen Mollie.

On Saturday, he decided to wash the car. It would make it look like

less of a wreck. But it wasn't outside
the house.

'Where is the car?' he asked.

'It broke down,' said Mum, folding
her arms. 'We have to wait till
Monday for the parts!'

'I don't believe it,' he shouted.
'You know I need the car this
weekend.'

'Grow up, will you,' she said,
glaring at him. 'Stop acting like a
spoilt brat!'

That made him wild. He paced up
and down the kitchen.

'This is the second time I've let my
mates down,' he shouted.

Jordan would never let him forget this. He would have to pretend he was ill. He practised a croaky voice then got on his phone to Jordan again.

'I think I've got the 'flu,' he croaked.

Jordan grunted. 'See yer, then,' he said.

It was harder ringing Mollie. He hadn't spoken to her since the day of his test.

'I'm sorry,' he croaked down the phone. 'I'm ill.'

'Hope you feel better soon,' Mollie said.

What did she think of him?

He spent a boring evening watching TV. What a way to spend Saturday night!

All the next week, Mum had one excuse after another. Gran was ill. The cat had to go to the vet. Mum needed the dentist.

Ryan was sick of lying to his friends. He was sick of waiting.

He made up his mind. He would have it out with Mum.

FOUR

That evening, he found Mum in the kitchen.

'I know your game,' he said. 'You don't want me to drive the car, do you?'

'Well ... I ... '

'I knew it!' he shouted. 'I look a complete loser, thanks to you.' He glared at her. 'Why?'

Mum frowned. 'I know the car is old, but it's still in one piece. I want to keep it that way.'

'I *have* passed my test!'

'Yes ... but ... I don't want you getting yourself killed.'

Ryan felt he was going to explode.

'You're only just beginning,' said Mum. 'The real test is when you get behind the wheel.'

'A test is a test. And I passed.' Ryan forced himself to calm down. If

he played it cool, maybe she would
see sense.

'I won't drink, if that's what you're
worried about,' he said.

'You'll drive too fast. Death on the
roads, that's what young drivers are.
Sorry, Ryan, but you're not having
the car.'

She turned away. Ryan stormed
out and marched down the alley
and into the street. He stared at the
car he wasn't allowed to drive.

The phone began ringing indoors.
The door opened and Kev stuck his
head out. 'It's for you!' he yelled.

Ryan dashed indoors, hoping it

would be Mollie. It was Jordan.

'Where are we going tonight?' he asked.

Ryan had to think quickly.

'How about a pizza,' he said.

'Yeah. Then we could see a movie,' said Jordan. 'There's a good one on at the multiplex.'

'All right. I'll ring Mollie.'

'Get her to bring her friend, Shaz, will you?' said Jordan. 'I fancy her.'

Ten minutes later, Ryan stood looking at himself in the bathroom mirror. Mollie had said she could come and she would bring Shaz.

He would just have to take the car.

FIVE

Ryan knew he shouldn't take Mum's keys, but he couldn't let the others down. He couldn't miss a date with Mollie. Not again.

At 7.15, he opened his bedroom

door and listened. He crept downstairs. Mum was watching TV in the front room.

Ryan tiptoed to the kitchen and took the keys off the hook. He was glad it was dark outside.

He unlocked the car door, climbed in and buckled up. Then he turned the key, put the car in gear and headed off down the road.

It was great being alone in the car. He was pleased he hadn't forgotten how to drive.

Jordan was waiting for him outside his house. He was grinning.

'So your mum let you have the car?' he said as he got in.

Ryan didn't answer. He didn't feel good about it, but he wasn't going to let on to Jordan. He felt excited about picking up Mollie. He wished the others weren't coming, but he would put up with them. It was going to be a great night.

The girls were waiting outside Mollie's house. Mollie looked great. His knees melted like chocolate.

'Hi,' he said.

'Hi,' said Mollie.

'Only two weeks late!' said Shaz.

Shaz bugged him, but he smiled at
Mollie.

Mollie smiled back. Then she ran
to the car and jumped in the back
with Shaz.

'All right,' laughed Shaz. 'Let's see
how fast you can go.'

Ryan gave her a filthy look. She
had always been a loud-mouth, but
she didn't have to make jokes about
his driving.

'Right,' he said. 'Here we go!'

SIX

Ryan felt great as he parked the car in the High Street.

In the pizza place, he sat next to Mollie. She slid up close to him.

'You're a brilliant driver,' she

whispered.

'Thanks.'

She looked up shyly from under those thick, long lashes. Ryan's heart raced.

Suddenly, Shaz broke into the spell.

'Come on, you love birds!' she laughed loudly.

Jordan sniggered. 'Yeah, we'll miss the start of the movie if you two don't put each other down.'

'I haven't touched her!' said Ryan.

'Yet!' laughed Shaz.

Ryan glanced at Mollie. Her face was scarlet. He guessed his was, too.

Mollie ran out to the car with Shaz. He didn't like Shaz. He wished he could have come alone with Mollie.

As he started the car, he wondered if Mum had noticed that the car was missing. She would be angry. He would have to face up to her when he got home.

The multiplex was five miles away. Ryan drove the car out of town and turned along the country road. He felt confident. Mum didn't know what she was talking about. Of course he could drive.

The road was dark and winding,

but Ryan knew it like the back of his hand. He could hear Mollie and Shaz giggling in the back. He smiled at Mollie in the mirror as a car's lights lit up their faces. She smiled back, then looked away.

Yes! He was on to a winner!

SEVEN

'Doesn't this car go any faster?'
Jordan asked.

'Of course it does,' said Ryan.

'What's it doing now?' laughed
Shaz. 'Twenty?'

Jordan looked at the speedo.

'Only forty,' he said.

'Only forty?' Shaz squawked like a parrot. Ryan wanted to wring her neck!

'You're a danger on the road when you drive too slowly,' Jordan teased.

'It's dark,' said Ryan. 'And there are so many bends.'

'Ooooo!' laughed Shaz. 'The boy's chicken!'

She was getting right up his nose.

'Mollie must think you're a real loser,' said Jordan.

At that moment, Ryan hated

Jordan almost as much as he hated
Shaz. But he couldn't let Mollie
think he was a loser.

'Of course I can drive faster,' he
snapped.

'If you dare!' shouted Shaz.

'Shut up, Shaz,' whispered Mollie.

'Prove it!' shouted Shaz.

That did it! Ryan suddenly felt
himself snap.

'Right!' he said. He pushed his
foot hard on the pedal. 'If you want
speed … '

Jordan leaned over to watch the
speedo.

'Forty-five … ' he said.

'Only forty-five?' squawked Shaz.

'Fifty … is that *it*?' jeered Jordan.

Ryan's heart began to beat faster. He was angry and a bit scared, but he was excited too.

'Fifty-five … ' said Jordan.

'Only fifty-five?' shrieked Shaz.

Ryan's foot pushed harder against the pedal. He would show them who was chicken!

'Sixty … ' shouted Jordan. 'Go, man, go!'

Suddenly, Ryan saw a sharp bend ahead. He was going too fast.

He jammed his foot on the brake. The lights of another car swung

round the bend and came towards them. He half closed his eyes, trying to see.

He heard tyres squealing and a horn honking. Then he heard Mollie scream as their car skidded sideways and hit the bank at the edge of the road.

'Look out!' Jordan yelled.

Crash!

The other car hit them side on.

Bang!

Ryan clung to the wheel and the girls screamed, as the car began to roll.

EIGHT

Suddenly, the car smacked up against a tree. The screaming stopped.

There was silence, apart from the hissing of the car engine.

Ryan felt dizzy. The pain in his legs took his breath away. He tried to move them, but they would not budge. They were trapped.

The steering wheel was right against his chest. How was he going to get out? What if there was a fire? They would all burn to death.

It suddenly hit him. He had driven too fast, like Mum said he would. 'Death on the road,' she had called it. He wished *he* was dead!

Mollie? Jordan? Shaz? Were they dead?

He switched on the internal light. There was blood oozing from a deep gash on Jordan's face. His eyes were closed.

Why did Mum have such an old car? A new one would have had air bags.

'Jordan?'

There was no answer.

'Mollie? Shaz?'

Not a sound.

He twisted round and looked over his shoulder. His head spun. There was blood everywhere, but no sound.

Silent as the grave.

Why did I have to be so stupid?

Torchlight blinded him.

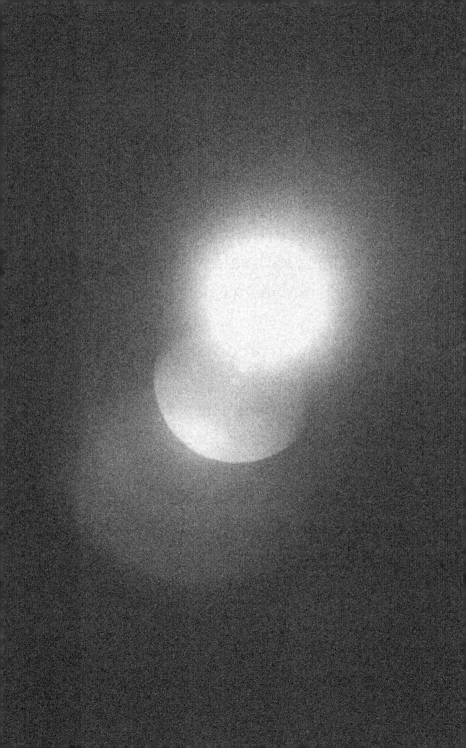

'Are you all right?' It was a man's voice.

Ryan felt too ill to answer. His legs were giving him hell.

'Oh, my God!' said a woman. 'I hope the ambulance gets here in time!'

There was a groan. It made Ryan jump. It was Jordan.

'You OK?' Ryan whispered.

'I'll live,' groaned Jordan. 'What about the girls?'

'I don't know,' said Ryan. He hated himself. He should have just told Jordan and Shaz to shut it and driven in his own way.

Then he heard a siren and saw flashing blue lights.

The pain was bad. There were voices and noise and lights …

… and Jordan groaning …

… and the pain in his legs …

… and the silence from the back of the car …

Then everything went black.

NINE

Ryan opened his eyes. He was lying flat on his back, looking up at a white ceiling. Where was he?

Then he knew. In hospital. His legs were killing him. He looked towards the bottom of the bed and saw a large dome over them.

Jordan? Mollie? Shaz? What had happened to them?

He tried to sit up, but fell back with a groan. A young man in uniform hurried towards him.

'So you're awake at last,' he said. 'I'm Martin, the charge nurse of this ward.' He pointed at the dome. 'Both legs badly broken – in plaster under there.'

Ryan had guessed they must be. He frowned. 'Where are the others?'

Martin didn't answer. 'Your mum's here,' he said.

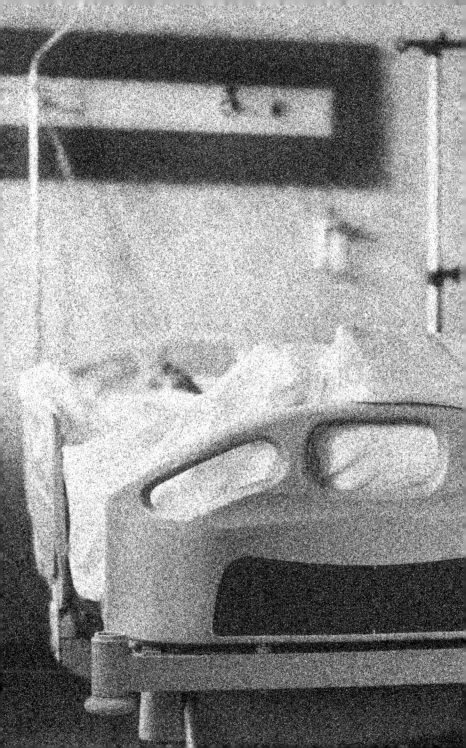

Ryan hadn't noticed Mum sitting there. He knew she must be angry, but he didn't want to hear what she was going to say. He didn't need telling he was an idiot. Or a murderer!

'Ryan.' Mum didn't sound angry. He sniffed. 'I'm sorry.'

'It's OK.' She touched his arm.

'The others?' he whispered, turning to look at her. Her face was red and blotchy, as if she had been crying. 'How bad?'

'Jordan's got cuts and bruises and a broken collar bone.'

'The girls?' he whispered. 'The

people in the other car? Mollie?'

Mum bit her lip and shook her head.

'Dead?' *Death on the roads!*

He *was* a murderer! Just because he wanted to impress Mollie. He turned away, unable to stop the tears.

TEN

'Not dead,' Martin said. 'Sharon and the people from the other car … they're out of danger. But Mollie … she's still unconscious.'

He'd never forgive himself for this.

Never!

He wiped his eyes with the back of his hand as Jordan came towards him. He had a bandage round his head and his arm was in a sling.

'My fault,' said Jordan.

'What?'

'*Your* fault?' said Mum. 'How?'

'Me and Shaz bugged Ryan something rotten,' said Jordan. 'Made him go faster. I'm sorry.'

Mum frowned, but she didn't speak.

'My dad's here,' said Jordan. 'He's come to take me home.'

When Jordan had gone Ryan

looked up at Martin. 'Where's Mollie?' he asked.

'Just along the corridor,' said Martin.

'Can I see her?'

Martin shrugged. 'All right,' he said. 'Just for a moment.'

Ryan lay back as Martin wheeled the bed out of the ward. Every jolt sent the pain shooting up his legs, but he clamped his teeth tight. Martin stopped by a door and pushed it open.

Mollie was lying on a bed, covered by a sheet. There were tubes and wires sticking out everywhere. A large bandage covered her head.

Her dad was sitting beside the bed. He glared at Ryan. If looks could kill, Ryan knew he would be stone dead. He wished he was.

Suddenly, he saw a movement.

'Look,' he whispered.

Mollie's eyelids fluttered and slowly, her eyes opened. Her dad jumped to his feet and leaned over her. She smiled up at him.

'Dad,' she whispered.

'Thank God!' said her dad.

Ryan squeezed his eyes tight shut and crossed his fingers, like he used to do when he was a kid.

Please let her be all right.

He knew he would have to face up to what he had done, but it would be a lot easier if Mollie was going to get better.

He sighed as Martin took him back to his ward. Then, as he began to drift off to sleep, in his head he seemed to hear his mum's words …

'The real test …'

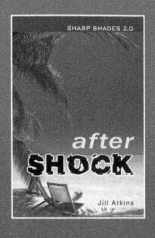

Aftershock

by Jill Atkins

It was the most beautiful place on Earth, a perfect holiday island. But that was before the tsunami. Now everything is smashed and broken. It leaves Maddy desperately searching for her family.

Ben's Room

by Barbara Catchpole

What do a zombie cockroach, a giant jellyfish and a shrinking room have in common? They're among the perils that Sam has to face after he storms out of his home and moves into an old flat.